C!CADAS

ASHLEY GISH

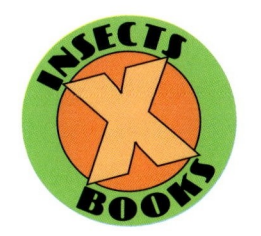

NORTH AMERICA
SOUTH AMERICA
EUROPE
AFRICA
ASIA
AUSTRALIA

CREATIVE EDUCATION • CREATIVE PAPERBACKS

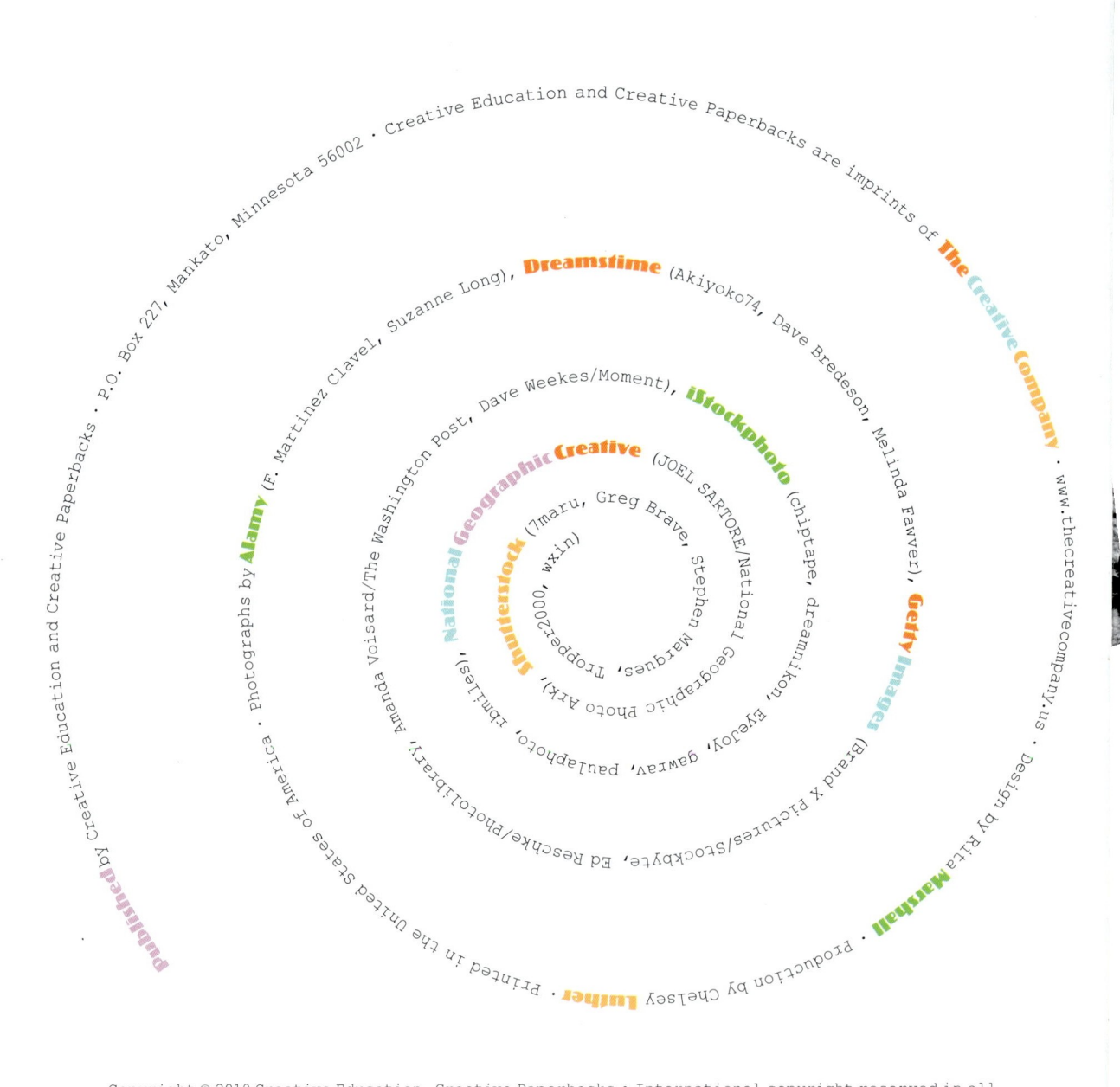

Published by Creative Education and Creative Paperbacks • P.O. Box 227, Mankato, Minnesota 56002 • Creative Education and Creative Paperbacks are imprints of The Creative Company • www.thecreativecompany.us

Design by Rita Marshall • Production by Chelsey Luther • Printed in the United States of America

Photographs by Alamy (F. Martinez Clavel, Suzanne Long), Dreamstime (Akiyoko74, Dave Bredeson, Melinda Fawver), Getty Images (Brand X Pictures/Stockbyte, Ed Reschke/Photolibrary, Amanda Voisard/The Washington Post, Dave Weekes/Moment), iStockphoto (chiptape, dreamnikon, Eyejoy, gawrav, paulaphoto, tbmalis), National Geographic Creative (JOEL SARTORE/National Geographic Photo Ark), Shutterstock (7maru, Greg Brave, Stephen Marques, Tropper2000, wxin)

Copyright © 2019 Creative Education, Creative Paperbacks • International copyright reserved in all countries. No part of this book may be reproduced in any form without written permission from the publisher. • Library of Congress Cataloging-in-Publication Data • Names: Gish, Ashley, author. • Title: Cicadas / Ashley Gish. • Series: X-Books: Insects. • Includes index. • Summary: A countdown of five of the most fascinating cicadas provides thrills as readers learn about the biological, social, and hunting characteristics of these loud, singing insects. • Identifiers: LCCN 2017060038 / ISBN 978-1-60818-989-2 (hardcover) / ISBN 978-1-62832-616-1 (pbk) / ISBN 978-1-64000-090-2 (eBook) • Subjects: LCSH: Cicadas—Juvenile literature. • Classification: LCC QL527.C5 G57 2018 / DDC 595.7/52—dc23
CCSS: RI.3.1-8; RI.4.1-5, 7; RI.5.1-3, 8; RI.6.1-2, 4, 7; RH.6-8.3-8
First Edition HC 9 8 7 6 5 4 3 2 1 • First Edition PBK 9 8 7 6 5 4 3 2 1

C!CADAS

CONTENTS

Xceptional **INSECTS** 5

Xciting **FACTS** 28

Xtreme **TOP 5 CICADAS**
- #5 **10**
- #4 **16**
- #3 **22**
- #2 **26**
- #1 **31**

Xasperating **CONFLICT** 24

Xtraordinary **LIFESTYLE** 18

Xemplary **SKILLS** 20

GLOSSARY
RESOURCES

INDEX 32

HEAD

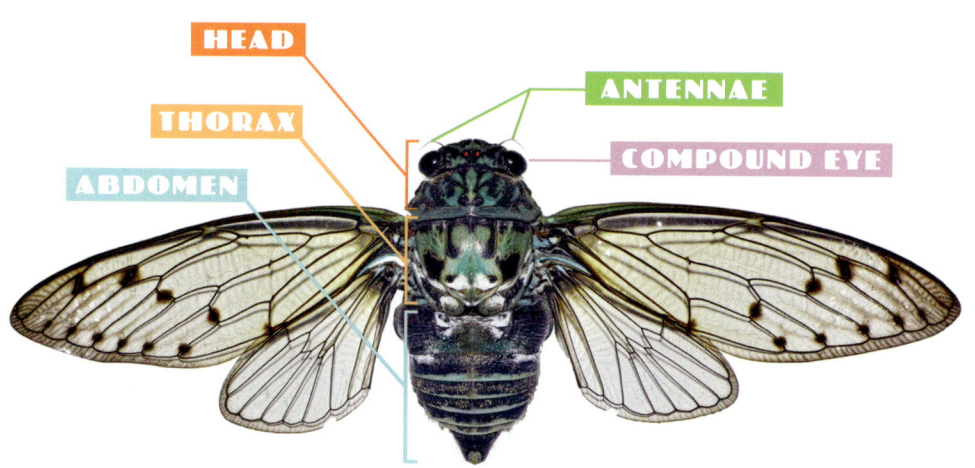

ANTENNAE

THORAX

COMPOUND EYE

ABDOMEN

XCEPTIONAL INSECTS

Cicadas are insects. Their sizes and sounds are extreme. Groups of them are heavy enough to bend and break tree branches. They are the loudest insects on Earth. More than 3,000 kinds of cicadas live around the world.

Cicada Basics

Cicada bodies are between one and two inches (2.5–5.1 cm) long. Like all insects, cicadas have six legs. Their body has three parts. These are the head, the thorax, and the abdomen. They have two pairs of wings.

All insects are protected by an exoskeleton. This hard armor is on the outside of their bodies. They also have **antennae** on their head. Cicadas use their antennae to sense their surroundings.

CICADAS OF THE WORLD

Cicadas live throughout the world in warm or tropical climates.

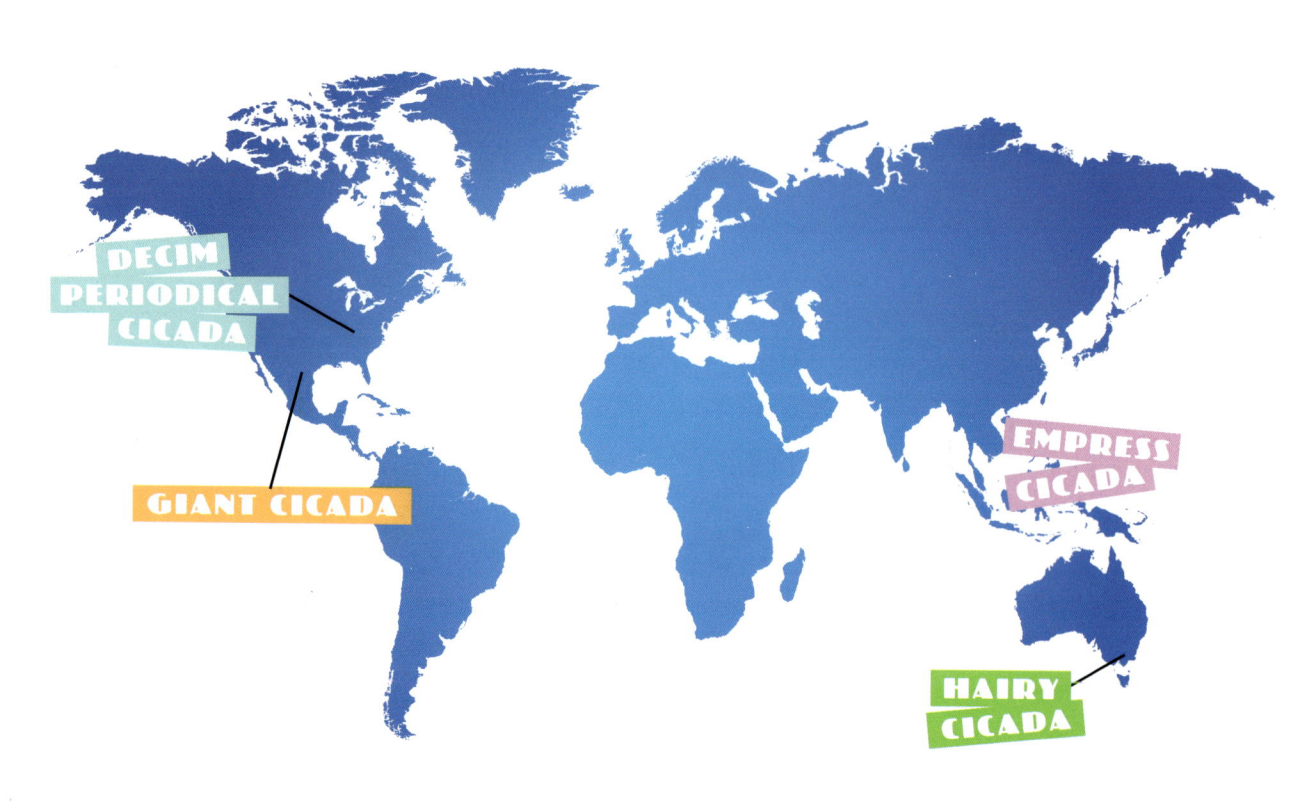

DECIM PERIODICAL CICADA

GIANT CICADA

EMPRESS CICADA

HAIRY CICADA

NORTH AMERICA

Almost 200 kinds of cicadas can be found in North America alone.

EMPRESS CICADA

DECIM PERIODICAL CICADAS

have 13- or 17-year life cycles, meaning they spend that much time underground before emerging!

HAIRY CICADAS

in Australia and Tasmania vibrate their bodies to communicate—they cannot call loudly like other cicadas.

EMPRESS CICADAS

are called "six o'clock cicadas" in Borneo because they start their noisy chorus at sunset.

wingspan — 8 inches (20.3 cm)

CICADA WINGS

Most wings are clear; some are colored or patterned.

Cicadas have better hearing than humans. Females can hear males up to a mile (1.6 km) away.

Cicadas have two **compound eyes**. They also have three smaller eyes centered on their head. These are called ocelli. They are used to detect light and darkness. Cicadas' eyes can be red, white, or multicolored.

Male cicadas "sing" by flexing drum-like **organs** in their bodies. These organs are called tymbals. They can flex from about 100 to nearly 500 times per second! Cicadas are the only insects in the world that can do this. Their songs can be heard half a mile (0.8 km) away.

8

All true bugs have sucking mouthparts.

TRUE ✗ BUGS

CICADA BASICS FACT

Some people call periodical cicadas locusts.

But real locusts are a type of grasshopper.

TOP FIVE XTREME CICADAS

Xtreme Cicada #5

Most-Threatened Species Most cicadas are plentiful. But three kinds are not. They are the Cassini, decim, and decula periodical cicadas. They all live in North America. The International Union for Conservation of Nature (IUCN) lists these **species** as near threatened. This means that they could die out. To protect these cicadas, people must try to avoid spraying bug poison and polluting the air and groundwater.

Many different animals eat cicadas, including squirrels, birds, bats, and even other insects.

Cicada Babies

Cicadas hatch from eggs. A female carves grooves in tree bark using a sharp spike at the end of her body. She lays up to 400 eggs inside these grooves. The eggs hatch in 6 to 10 weeks. Baby cicadas are called nymphs. As soon as they hatch, the nymphs fall to the ground and begin digging into the dirt.

A thin, shell-like body covering protects the nymphs. They burrow into the soil as deep as 18 inches (45.7 cm). Buried in the ground, they eat watery sap, called xylem, from tree roots.

The nymphs eat and grow for 1 to 17 years. Then they come out of the ground. At night, they crawl up the side of the nearest tree. Their shells split open, and the adult cicadas emerge. They now have wings and exoskeletons.

Different kinds of cicadas have different life cycles. Swamp cicada nymphs come out of the ground every year. But dog-day cicada nymphs stay underground for four years. And periodical cicada nymphs come out every 13 or 17 years!

up to 400 eggs — Females lay eggs

6 to 10 weeks — Nymphs hatch

1 to **17** years

Underground growth

live for **2** to **6** weeks

Emergence as adults

CICADA BABIES FACT

Periodical cicada nymphs come up from underground when the soil reaches 64 °F (17.8 °C).

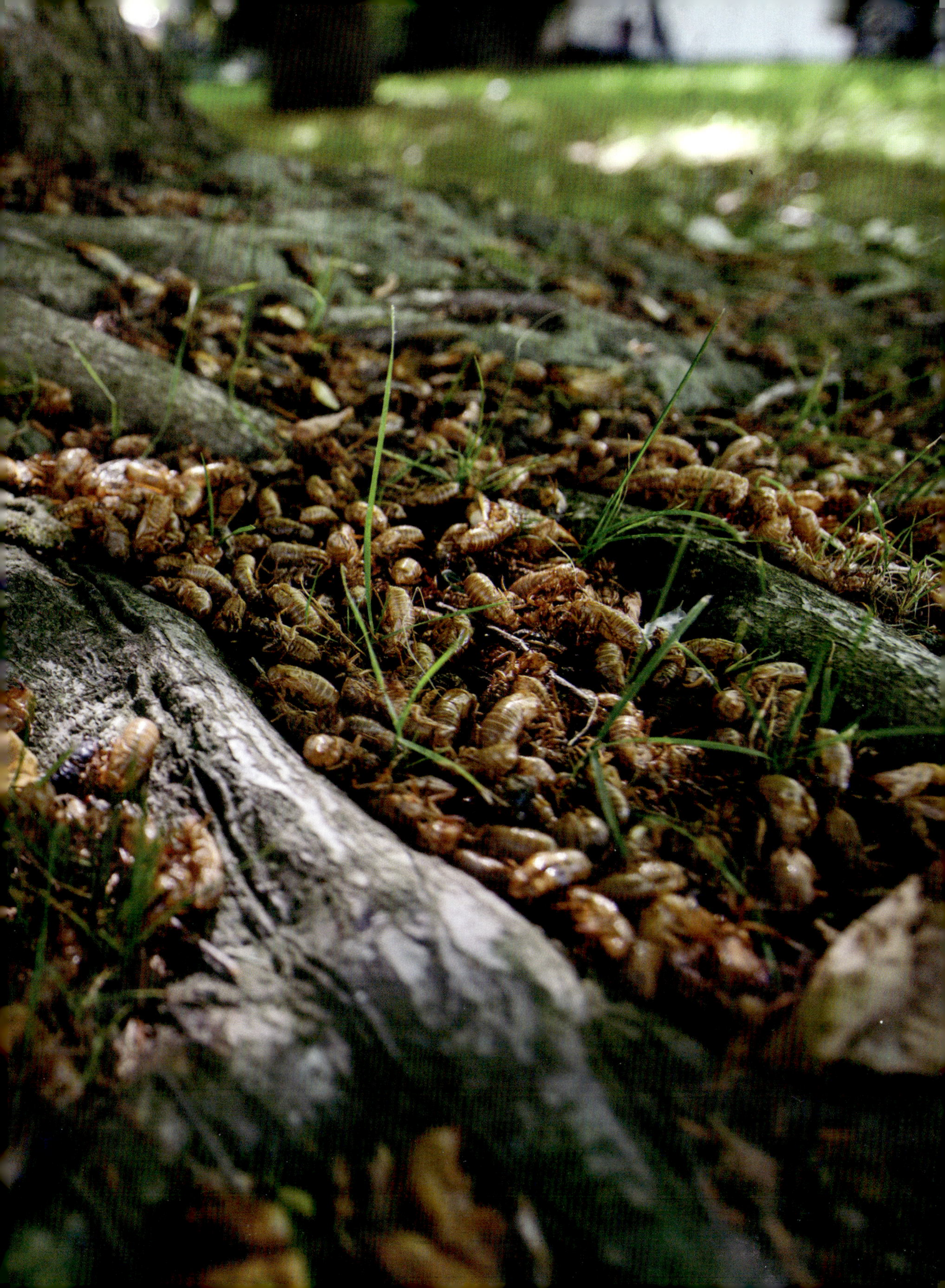

TOP FIVE XTREME CICADAS

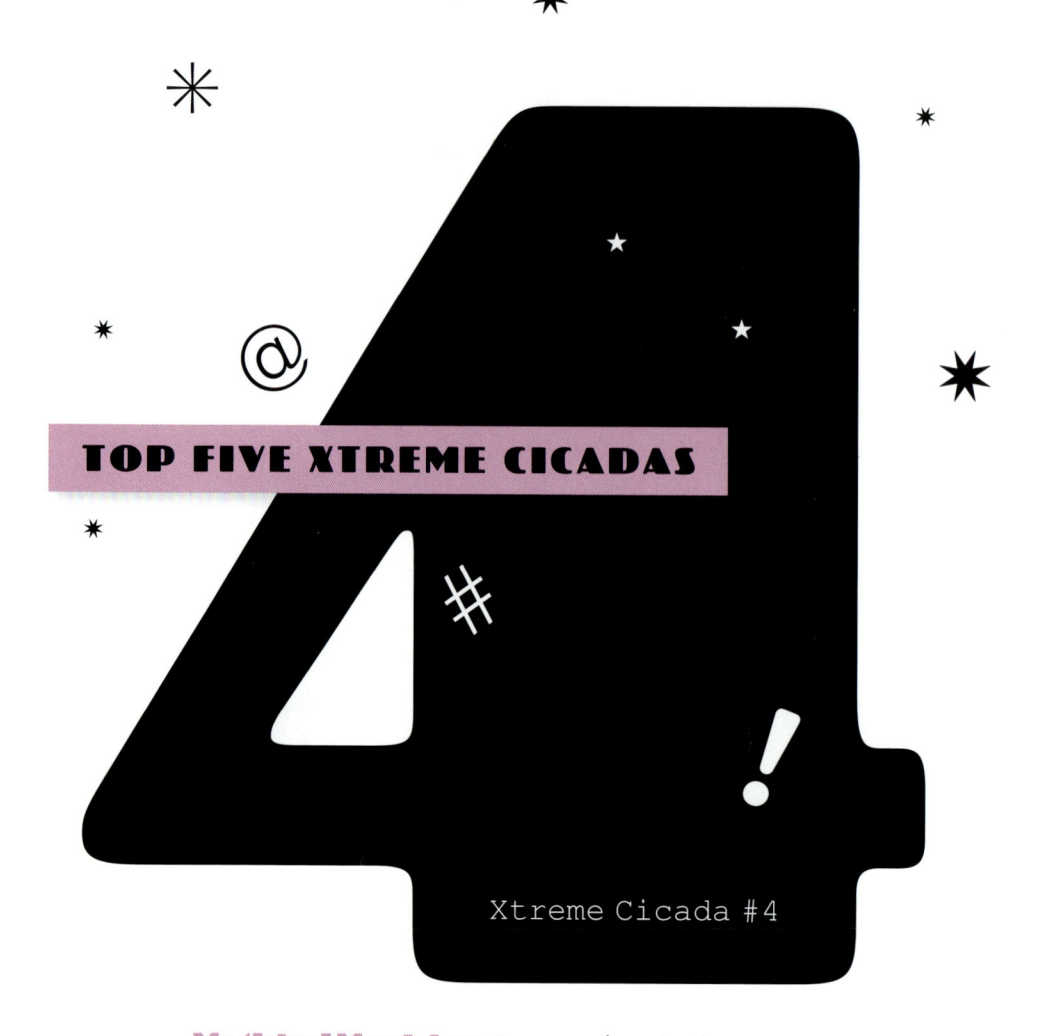

Xtreme Cicada #4

Mythical Musician In ancient Greece, a story was told about a musician named Eunomos. He played a stringed instrument called a cithara in music contests. Once, a string broke as he was playing. Eunomos thought he would surely lose the contest. Suddenly, a cicada landed on the cithara. The cicada made a sound just like that of the missing string. Eunomos finished the song and won the competition.

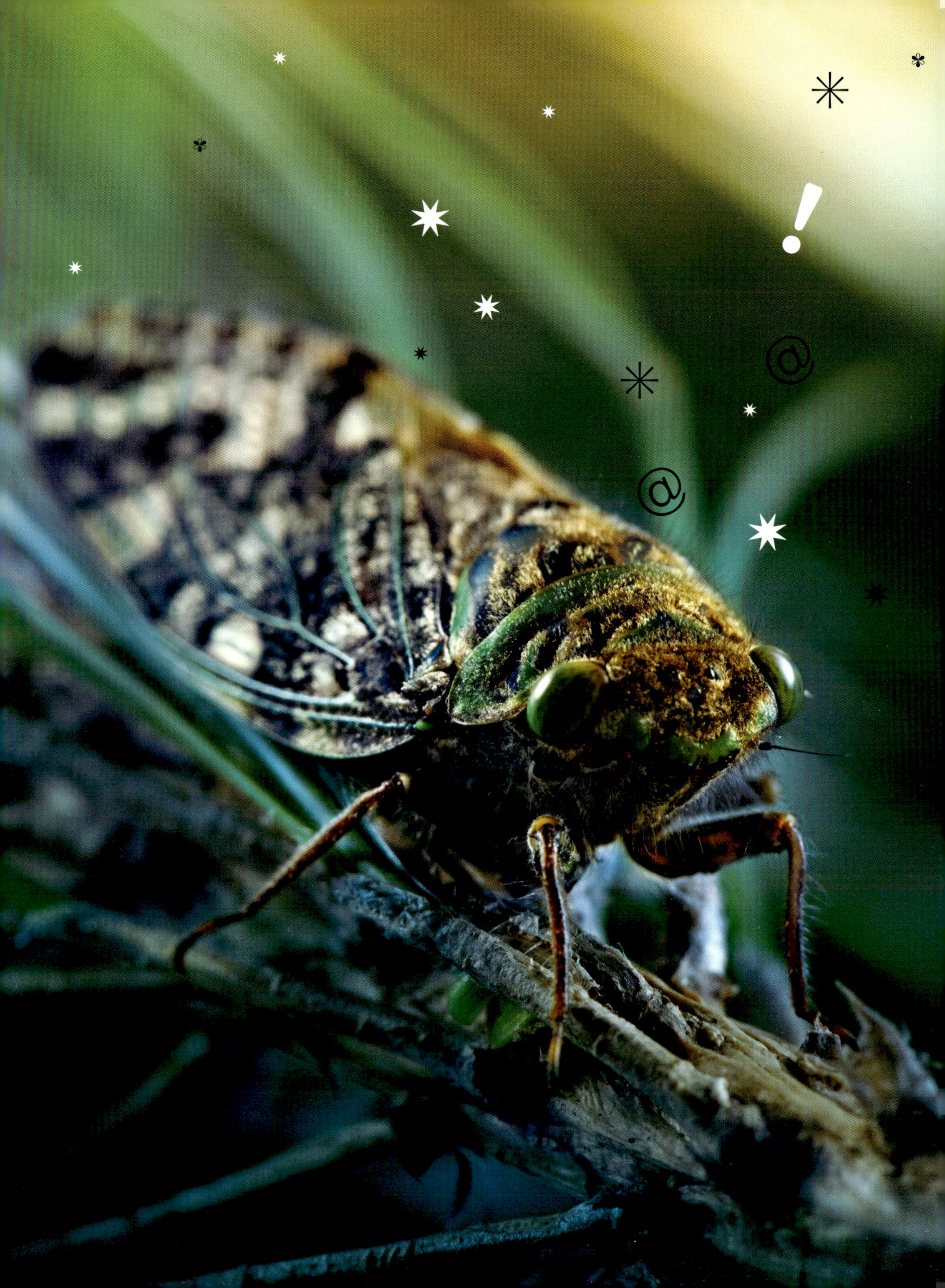

XTRAORDINARY LIFESTYLE

Most cicadas come together in huge swarms to find mates. There is safety in numbers. Their calls help them find each other. No two cicada species sound alike. Many people enjoy tracking these groups over the years.

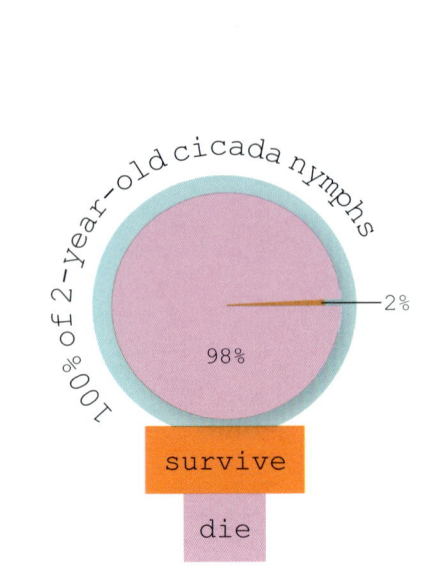

100% of 2-year-old cicada nymphs
- 98% survive
- 2% die

CICADA SOCIETY FACT

Broods of 13- and 17-year periodical cicadas hatch at the same time once every 221 years.

Nymphs shed and regrow their shells as they get bigger.

CICADA MOLTING

Cicada Society

Cicadas are large, gentle insects. They are not good at fighting. They have straw-like mouthparts for sucking sap. They cannot bite. Unlike bees and some ants, cicadas do not have stingers. But they have extreme power in numbers. Few other insects gather in swarms as large as cicadas'.

Males and females communicate by making different sounds. When people hear cicadas, they are hearing the males' songs. Some calls sound like a chainsaw slicing through wood. Others sound like chirps, followed by a long *eee-ooo-eee*. Many of these songs have been recorded and can be heard online.

Some species of cicada stay underground for 13 or 17 years. After they come out of the ground, they live for only a few weeks. Their time above ground is spent eating and looking for a mate. Cicada males do not fight each other. Females choose males based on their songs.

XEMPLARY SKILLS

A brood of nymphs hatches at the same time. They remain together underground. They emerge together, too. Cicada nymphs' legs are made for digging. They are shaped like shovels.

XEMPLARY SKILLS FACT

Some cicadas' calls are too high-pitched to be heard by the human ear.

A cicada's loudness is directly related to the size of its body. The bigger the cicada, the louder its song.

Hairs on cicadas' feet help them feel vibrations on the ground or in trees. Northern greengrocer and double drummer (pictured) cicadas group together to increase their noise level. Birds that normally eat cicadas will avoid large swarms. They cannot stand the noise!

Male cicadas have protective membranes covering their hearing organs. This keeps them from deafening themselves with their loud calls. Females make sounds in response to the males' calls. When they hear a male, they click their wings together.

TOP FIVE XTREME CICADAS

Xtreme Cicada #3

Delicious Dish Shandong is a cooking style in China. A popular Shandong dish is *zha jinchan*—deep-fried golden cicadas. People go out at night and use flashlights to spot cicadas. They use bamboo poles to knock the sleeping cicadas out of trees. Then they sell the cicadas to local restaurants. One golden cicada is worth about a nickel. A family working together can catch about 1,000 cicadas each night.

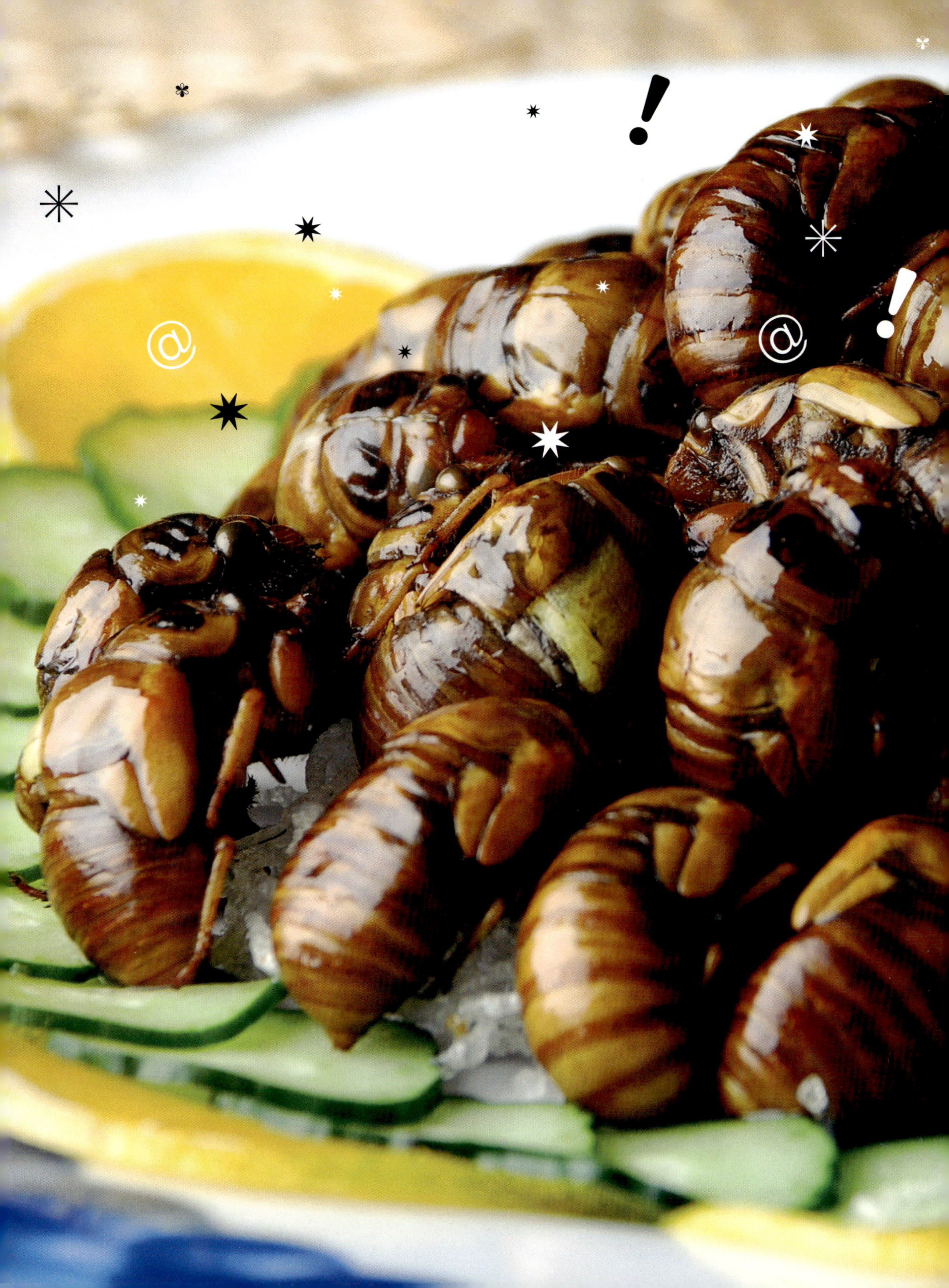

XASPERATING CONFLICT

People and cicadas interact in many ways. One way is through sound. Female cicadas think lawn mowers and power tools sound like male cicadas. For this reason, they may land on people who are working in their yards.

Cicada Survival

Cicadas are good for the environment. When cicada nymphs come out of the ground, the tunnels they leave behind introduce air to the earth. Dead cicadas add **nutrients** to the soil. But female cicadas can damage young trees. Branches may split when female cicadas lay eggs in them.

Some human activities, such as paving roads and spraying weed killers, are deadly to cicadas. Scientists track the life cycles of periodical cicada broods. There are 12 different 17-year broods. There are just three 13-year broods. Each brood is assigned a roman numeral. Brood XIX is expected to emerge in 2024. Research is important to help protect cicadas.

Periodical cicada broods can number as many as 1.5 million per acre (0.4 ha).

They live for only two to six weeks above ground. **Most** of their lives are spent underground. **Nymphs** of species that reproduce yearly spend four to seven years underground. **Periodical** cicadas live underground for up to 17 years. **They** usually come out in late May or early June. **They** emerge from June through August. **Adult** cicadas must reproduce quickly.

CICADA SURVIVAL FACT

If soil is too wet, nymphs build mud tubes. The tubes stick up from the ground and protect the nymphs.

TOP FIVE XTREME CICADAS

Xtreme Cicada #2

Impressive Size The empress cicada of Southeast Asia is the biggest cicada. Its body is about 2.8 inches (7.1 cm) long. Its wings can spread up to eight inches (20.3 cm) wide. Being the largest cicada, it may also be the loudest. Unfortunately, its call has never been recorded, so we cannot know for sure. Scientists weighed a dried empress cicada. It weighed as much as two M&M's® candies.

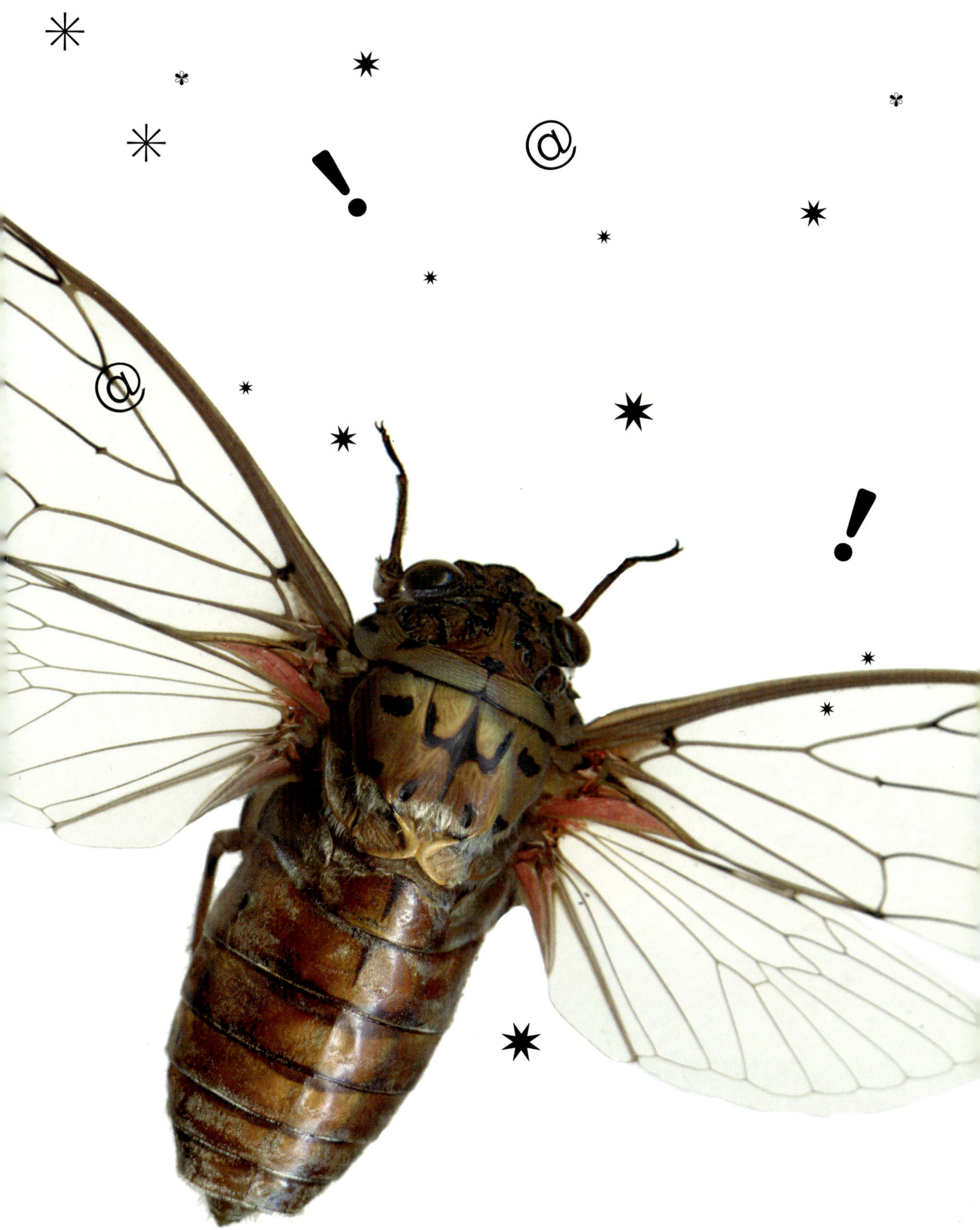

XCITING FACTS

After they drink, cicadas pass unused watery sap out of their bodies in tiny streams.

Females lay eggs on branches that are one-quarter to one-half inch (0.6–1.3 cm) thick.

The papery brown shells that nymphs shed are called exuviae (ig-ZOO-vee-ee).

Australia's hairy cicadas have changed very little from cicadas that lived millions of years ago.

Colossocossus giganticus was a cicada that lived more than 120 million years ago.

Nymphs can fall prey to young feather-horned beetles underground.

Cicadas wiggle their mouthparts to get a good angle for piercing plants and sucking sap.

Dog-day cicadas have transparent wings with green veins that blend in with leaves.

The Kempfer cicada has speckled wings that help it blend in with tree bark.

Scientists have discovered some 3,000 different kinds of cicada, but only 1,500 have been named.

About 190 cicada species can be found in North America.

Newly emerged adults are whitish. After a few days, their exoskeletons darken.

Nymphs are fossorial creatures. This means they are specialized for digging.

Cicada killer wasps

sting cicadas.

Then they carry the dead insects to their nest to feed their young.

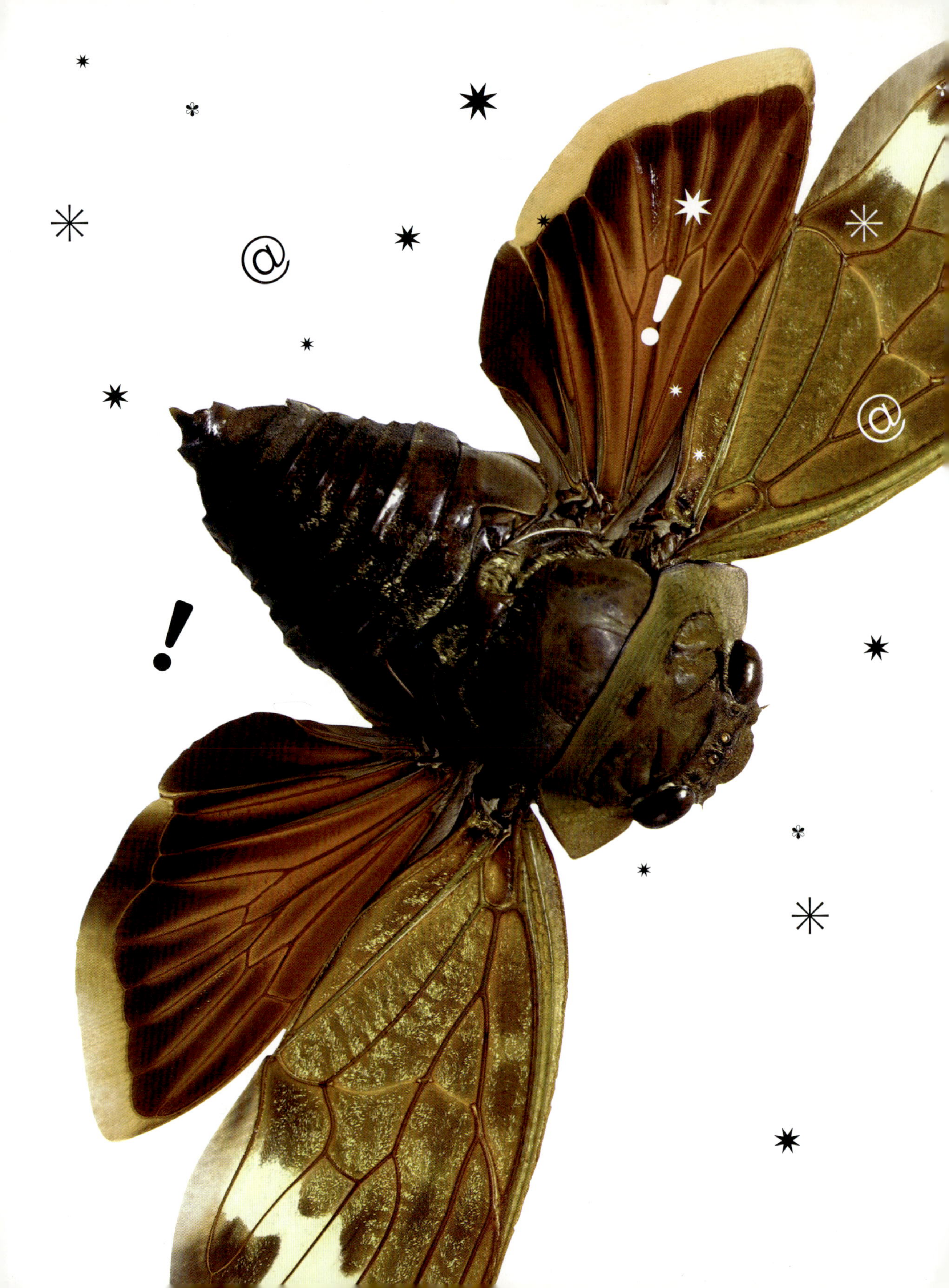

TOP FIVE XTREME CICADAS

Xtreme Cicada #1

Rising Decibels North America's Walker's cicada makes the loudest burst of sound. It can reach 109 decibels. This alarm warns of predators. The African cicada (left) makes the loudest constant sound. Its noise level reaches nearly 107 decibels. That is louder than a snowmobile or motorcycle! Standing next to an African cicada for too long could be dangerous. Doctors say that steady sounds above 85 decibels can damage hearing.

GLOSSARY

antennae – body parts that protrude from the head and are used for sensing surroundings

compound eyes – those made up of many parts that see in many directions at once

membranes – thin, bendable structures that separate different parts of a living thing's body

nutrients – substances that give a living thing energy and help it grow

organs – parts of a living being that perform specific tasks in the body

species – a group of living beings that are closely related

RESOURCES

BBCWorldwide. "Amazing Cicada life cycle - Sir David Attenborough's Life in the Undergrowth - BBC wildlife." YouTube video, 5:17. Posted October. 2008. https://www.youtube.com/watch?v=tjLiWy2nT7U.

"Cicada." Bug Facts. http://www.bugfacts.net/cicada.php.

Hoover, Gregory A., Sr. "Periodical Cicada." Penn State College of Agricultural Sciences. http://ento.psu.edu/extension/factsheets/periodical-cicada.

Kritsky, Gene. *In Your Backyard: Periodical Cicadas*. Columbus: Ohio Biological Survey, 2016.

INDEX

diet 12, 19, 28

eggs 12, 24, 28, 32

mates 18, 19, 21

nymphs 12, 14, 19, 20, 24, 25, 28

physical features 5, 8, 9, 12, 19, 20, 21, 26, 28

predators 11, 21, 22, 28, 31

sounds 5, 7, 8, 16, 18, 19, 20, 21, 24, 26, 31

species 5, 6, 7, 9, 10, 12, 14, 18, 19, 21, 22, 24, 25, 26, 28, 31

Male cicadas can fly faster than females, which are weighed down by eggs.